Close Call

by
Lucinda Ray

Watermill Press

Printed in the United States of America

Illustrations by Jim Odbert

ISBN 0-89375-697-0

Contents

"How do you knock down half a bridge?"

Danger at the Bridge

"How do you knock down half a bridge?" Shane shook his head in disbelief.

"It beats me," was all Hap could offer.

The two boys stood on their fishing bridge. It had been destroyed beyond description. Large chunks had been broken loose and dumped into the lake.

"If it were an old wooden bridge, I could understand," Shane said. "You could just kick it apart. But this is cement and stone, more than a hundred years old. It's solid."

"Beats me," Hap said again.

The bridge was called Bell Bridge, because it was built over a narrow place on Bell Lake. Once, it had led to a small beach with a picnic area. Now the beach and picnic area were gone. Mostly, the bridge was just a peaceful place for fishing.

The boys set up their fishing gear. But it wasn't the same. Their beautiful spot had been turned into a dump.

Finally, Shane said, "Let's go. The place is ruined."

Hap made a face. "I hate to just get chased off," he said. "There must be something we can do."

"What?" Shane wanted to know.

"Maybe we can catch whoever ruined the bridge," Hap said. "Or, at least we can find out who they are. I figure, if they had fun doing this much damage, they'll be back for more."

"You mean we wait for them?" Shane asked. "Then what?"

"Then, I don't know," Hap said. "We'll see. We'll play it by ear."

They returned that night with sleeping bags and flashlights. Their plan was to stay hidden in the bushes. Then they would see what more they could do.

It seemed like a long wait and a cold

one. The boys crawled into their sleeping bags. They waited some more, then dozed off.

Suddenly, there was a loud bang! The boys were jolted awake. Bright lights were shining nearby. Looking out of the bushes, Hap and Shane saw a car. Its lights were shining on the bridge. There was a splash and some laughter. The boys could see three men on the bridge. The men were pushing large chunks of rock off the bridge and into the lake.

Hap and Shane were shaking now. It was part cold and part nerves. The vandals were out there. What could the boys do?

The vandals were making wisecracks. "Pow! And down she goes," one laughed.

They worked on the bridge for a few minutes. Then they ran off. *"Blam!"* There was another explosion.

"They're blowing it up!" Hap said. "They have small charges, like big firecrackers or something. Let's stop them."

"No way," Shane said. "You go for the police. I'll see if I can keep them here till you get back."

"Fat chance of that," Hap said. "They'll have the bridge down and be gone before I can get back."

"Trust me," Shane said. "I'll think of something. Now go quietly so they don't hear you."

Hap slipped off into the darkness. He went so quietly that Shane got an idea.

He swallowed hard. Then he cried

out from the bushes. "Hey, fatheads! Haven't you got anything better to do?"

The three on the bridge froze. "Let's get out of here," one said.

"Nah," said another. "That's a kid's voice. Let's get him." In a rush, they headed for the bushes where they heard the voice. But, when they got there, Shane was gone.

"Out here, jerks!" Shane was now at the end of a little path. The vandals dashed after the voice once again. The leader tripped and fell. The others were right behind, and fell in a heap on top of him. Shane had tied a long vine across the path. Cursing, they scrambled to their feet and looked around.

"The car!" one of them screamed.

The car was moving. In the confusion, Shane had slipped away to the car. He shifted it into neutral. Then he got behind and pushed. It was on a slight slope, so it moved easily.

As Shane faded into the darkness, there was a loud splash. The car plunged into the lake and sank. Two of the men had had enough and ran off. The other one stayed. Shane figured he must be the owner of the car.

When the police came with Hap, the guy was easy enough to catch. He was sitting on a rock and staring into the lake. When he saw the police, he jumped up and started screaming.

"My car!" he shouted. "The kid ruined my car!" Tears were streaming down his face.

The car plunged into the lake.

"So that's how it feels, huh?" a policeman said. "Let's all go down to the station and talk about it."

Hap and Shane felt like heroes. But they weren't at all sure that they liked the feeling.

The Pictures Came Out Great!

I hate to admit it. But, sometimes, my parents are right. For instance, they dragged me along on their vacation trip, even after I had lined up a summer job. I tried to get out of it. I tried begging. I tried sulking. I tried saying "No." Nothing worked.

There was a time when I would have jumped to join them. But I'm older now. I've got other interests. Besides, the last time I was away, my girl started going out with someone else. So you can see why I wasn't too keen to leave again. But, as I said, this time my parents were right.

As a bribe, they gave me a camera. I guess I should mention that my parents take pictures as a sideline. They write about these trips for a travel magazine. My dad says it's a good way for a teacher to see the world. It seems to me that all he sees are maps and trail-markers. He spends a lot of time getting lost. But I guess he likes it. My mom is a real health nut. She loves hiking.

As a bribe, my parents gave me a camera.

So here I was, staggering up a mountain pass with a thirty-pound backpack. I was already lonesome for my new girlfriend, Jane.

This year's trip was to Glacier National Park, in Montana. Even a grouch like me loved the scenery right away. The mountains have ice and snow on them all year round. The lakes are bright blue. My dad was going crazy, collecting purple rocks for school. My mom was clicking away with her camera. I was slowly figuring out how mine worked. And, of course, I was writing postcards to Jane.

We planned to hike up to a glacier and camp out. We were way above the tree line. It felt strange to be up so high. I was smearing suntan lotion on

17

my nose and ears. At the same time, I was watching my footing across the snow. We had to stop every ten minutes to rest and catch our breath. The oxygen is a lot thinner at 8000 feet.

"Look at this purple flower. It's growing right out of the snow!" exclaimed my mom. "I've never seen one like this. Hmm-m-m. The guidebook says it's *bitterwort*. Very rare, too." She grabbed her camera out of her pack. I leaned back into a bush and tried to relax.

"Hey, look at the fuzzy white fur all over this bush," I said. "Do you think polar bears live all the way up here?" I was kidding about the bears. But Dad got really excited. He started collecting samples of the white stuff. Mom finished snapping the flower, and we all started on again.

This time, it was my turn to set the pace. I guess I was showing off, because Mom and Dad weren't right behind me anymore. I slowed down a bit and reached for my camera. I was trying to find just the right picture to take. I wanted Jane to be impressed. I hunched down to focus. The trail stretched across the snow and turned around the edge of a cliff. Then it dipped out of sight.

I pushed the button, and the shutter clicked. As I started to refocus, a great, sharp-horned mountain goat stared through the lens at me. I blinked. Two goats! I rubbed my eyes and set down the camera. Was the thin air getting to me? When I opened my eyes again, two big goats and a

I took pictures as fast as I could.

baby goat were looking me over. They seemed as surprised as I was.

Slowly, I reached for the camera again. Snap. Advance the film. Snap. Advance. I took pictures as fast as I could. I fumbled in my pack for my telephoto lens. I wanted some close-up shots. The movement of my hand must have scared the goats. They disappeared back around the curve in the trail.

I stopped for a second. Should I try to fit on the new lens? Or should I run after them? I decided to run. I dropped my pack and took off.

The trail was slippery. I slid across the rocks and ice, and grabbed on to a bush to keep from falling. That's when I realized what that white fuzzy stuff was. The mountain goats were

*The trail was blocked by the
other big goat.*

shedding. Their fur clung to all the bushes.

I came to the curve in the trail. A narrow path was cut into the wall of the cliff. The drop-off below the trail was hundreds of feet. I edged along the wall, trying not to look down.

Then I froze in my tracks. Twenty feet ahead were the sharp horns of a frightened mother goat. She had planted herself in the middle of the trail. Her kid was behind her. I turned back. But the trail was blocked by the other big goat. I picked up a rock. Then I saw how useless one rock would be if either goat decided to charge. I set down the rock and took pictures instead. At least my parents would know how I died when they developed the film.

Suddenly, the goats disappeared. Maybe they didn't like clicking noises, because as quickly as they had appeared, they were gone. Had I been dreaming? I checked my camera. No, I wasn't dreaming. I had taken thirty pictures in the last few minutes.

My parents appeared a couple of minutes later. My dad was grumbling because I left my backpack in the middle of the trail. My mom scolded me for using up film so fast. But I think they were just glad to find I was safe. So was I.

As soon as we got home, I took that roll of film to be developed. The pictures of the goats came out great. Jane was very impressed. So was the man at the camera shop. He suggested I enter them in a photo contest. Guess what? I won first prize. The prize money amounted to more than I would have earned at my summer job. So, as I said, I hate to admit it. But I sure am glad my parents dragged me along on that trip.

A Fatal Slip

Meg leaned out over the waves. The wind had picked up. The boat tilted sharply.

"Keep on hiking!" shouted Don. "Good going! This won't last long."

Meg guessed that leaning was called "hiking" on a sailboat. Don used so many words she didn't understand. Ten minutes ago, she had been

Meg leaned out over the waves.

sunning herself. Don's sailing partner had not shown up. The race rules said there must be two people in each boat. Don had begged her to join him. So here she was, in her first sailboat race.

Don pointed to three floating markers. They made a triangle. "We sail around the black buoy," he explained. "Next, we sail around the orange, then the yellow. The problem in a sailboat is that..."

Meg listened with only one ear. She was looking at the other boats and at the shore. The view from out here was something else! Usually she was *in* the water, instead of *on* it. Meg was a swimmer. She spent many hours each day working out in the pool. In the YMCA pool, the world is small and easy to control. There are no waves.

You can see the bottom. There are no surprises. Out here, everything seemed different, even the water. Now Meg understood what people meant about getting a different *perspective*. She was getting a whole new view of the water.

"Pull in on this rope. Sheet in," called out Don. Meg pulled, and then she watched. The boats were crowded together. But Don steered through them without hitting any. Sails snapped in the wind. People were shouting orders. The boats were rounding the black marker now and heading for the orange one.

They started moving much faster. Meg had to hike out even farther, to keep the boat balanced. She saw other crew members do the same.

A boy was standing up in one of the boats.

A boy was standing up in one of the boats ahead of them. He was trying to free a line. The rope was caught on the wrong side of the sail. Just as he reached out, a gust of wind came up. All the boats tilted over. The boy's foot slipped. He fell into the water.

Meg heard a crack as he fell. His head must have hit the deck. Meg acted at once. She had been taught to save swimmers in trouble. So she kept her eyes on the spot where he fell. When he didn't come up, she shouted to Don.

"Don! The boy is in trouble. He's still down! I'm going after him!"

Meg checked to make sure she was clear of the other boats. Then she dove in. She swam to the spot where he had entered the water. But there

Meg dove into the water.

was no sign of him.

Now Meg was worried. Three or four minutes had passed since the accident. She made a surface dive, looking for him underwater. Between dives, she could see boats turning back to help. Don sailed close by. He was standing up, looking down into the water.

"He's on your left about four feet. No, a little farther. Right there! Good luck!"

Meg dove under the choppy surface. In the gray-green light underwater, she found him.

The hours which followed were a blur in Meg's memory. She tried her hardest to revive the boy. She did everything she had been trained to do. She never stopped until the doctor took over.

But it hadn't worked. The boy was dead. Meg couldn't quite believe it yet. She sat on the dock. She pictured in her mind's eye the lifesaving books she had read. She thought about the lifesaving courses she had taken. Life-saving, they called it. No one ever thought about failing to save a life. She shivered in the warm sun. What good had all those books and courses been? Saving lives in books was easy. There was always a happy ending. But real lifesaving had a different perspective.

"He was already dead."

The voice above her made her jump in surprise. She hadn't heard Don coming. Meg looked up at him and then back toward the water.

"I know," she sighed.

"No, I mean even before you reached him. The doctors say he died at once, when he hit his head on the deck. There was nothing anyone could have done."

Meg thought about this news.

"Thanks for coming to tell me, Don. Knowing that helps a little. I've been thinking it was my fault he died."

"Your fault?" spluttered Don. "Why, from my point of view, you were the only one who knew what to do. The rest of us just sailed around in circles."

Meg was silent for a moment. She looked out over the lake: the water, the boats, the people. From the dock, the lake looked very big. The sailboats and their crews looked very small. *Those little people are at the mercy of that big lake*, Meg thought. This was another perspective — another view.

Finally, her courage returned.

"Don, could I sail with you again sometime?"

White Water Peril

"Don't be a fool, Chuck! It's probably junk!" Andy knew he wasn't going to change Chuck's mind. But he had to try. He crawled after Chuck, shouting.

"Look how fast the water's moving! What if you do get out there without killing yourself? What then? You'll never get back."

Chuck wasn't listening. He just kept picking his way over the rocks and tree stumps along the edge of the river. It was early April. The river was boiling. Chuck kept his eye on a silvery flash. Every spring, he found lots of good stuff in this river: bikes, hubcaps, fenders. One time, he even found a boat trailer. But it was too big to drag out by himself. It finally washed downstream. Someone else probably got it.

The snow and ice had been torn off the rocks by the rush of spring water. Andy couldn't let Chuck stay out there by himself. And he knew he couldn't talk Chuck into turning back. So he scrambled after him.

"Hey, Chuck! Wait! Don't be an idiot!"

Chuck turned and waved. "I think it's a canoe. What luck! Hurry up!"

Andy hurried to catch up. Chuck might try something crazy, like walking out into the flooding river. He could see now what Chuck was after. It *did* look like a canoe. And it seemed to be in one piece. He reached Chuck just as he was taking off his jacket.

"You aren't going swimming out there! That's instant death!" hollered Andy.

"I'm not *that* stupid," answered Chuck. "I'm just trying to pull the canoe in to shore, that's all. I was trying to use my jacket as a kind of rope. But it's too short. Look. The canoe is caught by that rope tied around the seat. It looks like the rope is tangled on this tree." Chuck was inching out

39

Chuck was inching out on a big dead tree which stuck out into the river.

on a big dead tree which stuck out into the river. "Now, I could untangle
the canoe rope. But unless I'm tied onto the tree, the canoe will pull me out
into the river when it comes loose."

"Hey! Just a minute—wait!" cried
Andy. He felt like a broken record. He
kept saying "Wait!", and Chuck kept
right on going.

Before Andy knew it, he was out on
the old tree himself. Using their belts,
he strapped Chuck to a limb. Soon,
Chuck was busy hauling in the canoe.
The river was pulling on it just as
hard. Twenty minutes passed before
Chuck finally grabbed hold of its side.

"OK, Andy," said Chuck. "I'll hold
the canoe. You crawl back to shore.
Take the end of the rope with you. Tie
it somewhere good and tight. Then I'll

let go of the rope out here. I can unstrap myself and crawl to shore. Then we can both pull the canoe in."

He sure figures all the angles, thought Andy. In another twenty minutes, they had the canoe almost on shore.

They thought they had it. But then, the canoe wedged itself between some rocks and logs. They crawled out on the rocks again. Andy held on to a limb. Chuck held on to Andy and tried to push the canoe free with his feet. All of a sudden, Andy's feet slipped. He fell toward Chuck. Both boys toppled into the canoe. The force of their fall pushed the boat off the rocks. And their fall also snapped the rope which held the canoe fast to shore.

The boys were so surprised, they

couldn't move for a few seconds. Then, before they knew it, the canoe was far from shore. They were heading down the raging river!

Andy was afraid to move. The slightest movement might tip the canoe. The river water splashed into the boat.

Chuck lifted his head. In less than a minute, the canoe had shot downstream almost to the highway bridge. Chuck waved one arm wildly. He hoped a car might spot them and somehow save them. But no cars were in sight.

"If we flip, should we hang on to the canoe or try to swim?" gasped Andy.

"If we flip, we're dead," shouted Chuck grimly.

Suddenly, they lurched forward as

They were heading down the raging river!

the canoe smashed into a snag of dead trees. For a moment, both boys were motionless. They were waiting to drown, or to be torn further downstream. Slowly, it dawned on them that their voyage was over. Chuck poked his head up again.

"We're saved! We're saved!" he shouted. "In another ten minutes, we'll be on shore. What a piece of luck!"

"That is, if we don't shake the boat loose first," Andy warned.

"True. But at least we have a chance," said Chuck. "You hold on to me while I climb up. That way, if the canoe slips, I can pull you up." Andy was too scared to argue. So he held on to Chuck's ankle. A few seconds later, Chuck was sitting upon a branch, pulling Andy up beside him.

"Grab the rope," said Chuck. "We'll pull the canoe to shore with us."

"Nothing doing! I'm going home. This is one treasure you'll have to do without."

Chuck knew when he was pushing their friendship too far. "Just kidding, just kidding," he grinned. "Head for shore, Andy. White-water canoeing never did interest me. I think I'll let this canoe drift down to the fellow who got that boat trailer last year."

My Last Race— I Promise!

The morning sun danced off their ten-speed bikes. Reporters from the local radio station crowded around the starting line. They were interviewing the bikers. The race was about to begin.

"How long have you been racing, Jim?" asked one of the reporters.

"Well, this is my first season. I just entered to see how I liked it."

"And how long have the rest of you been racing?"

"Four years," answered one racer.

"Two years," answered another.

"Clear the way," instructed a voice on a bullhorn. The reporters moved back.

Allen leaned toward Jim. "If you're just in it for fun, how about taking it easy, Jim? I've been training for more than two years. If I win today, I might have enough money for college."

The starting gun cracked before Jim could reply. The police kept traffic clear as the bikers raced down Main Street.

Mike, a skinny blond, shifted gears.

He wanted to take advantage of the downgrade. *Just think about passing the guy in front of you,* he told himself. He had to win some money in this race. If not, he wouldn't even be able to pay for the parts he had put into his bike.

Paul Kenyon paid little attention to the other racers. He had won almost every race around here during the last four years. He had promised his wife that this would be his last race. He wanted it to be the best race of his career.

The route was marked with red arrows along the roadside. As the racers neared the edge of town, the police escort honked and drove off. The bikers began to spread out in single file.

Paul was in the lead. He always

Paul Kenyon is in the lead.

tried to get out in front early. Mike, Allen, and Jim were fighting for second place. The route led into the hills and back roads outside of town. The red arrows would lead the racers in a fifteen-mile circle.

Paul's wife, Alice, waited until the bikers were out of sight. Then she got into her car. She switched on the car radio as she drove toward the finish line.

"Our reporter for *Sports Today* brings you a live report on the annual bike race. Well, sports fans, Paul Kenyon is in the lead. It's hard to see who's in second place. A tight cluster of bikers seems to be . . ."

Alice Kenyon smiled. If Paul won this race, maybe he really would give up racing. Alice began to dream about vacations and Saturday picnics. She pictured a dining room that didn't look like a bicycle repair shop.

Out on Route 86, the hot sun was heating tempers. Mike and Jim had been in second and third place. But, in fighting for an edge, they missed the red arrow which marked the turnoff onto Route 7. They sped on down Route 86. Mike could see ahead for a mile or more. Paul was nowhere in sight. There were no red arrows. He wheeled his bike around angrily.

"What a bummer! We missed the turnoff!" he shouted at Jim.

"Watch where you're going!" yelled Jim. He swerved to avoid crashing into Mike.

"That's what I should have been doing back there, instead of . . ."

A helicopter buzzed overhead. It drowned out their shouts.

"This is *Sports Today* with another live report on the bike race. Here we are, sports fans, high above the race. Looks like numbers 6 and 10 have taken a detour. Too bad. Paul Kenyon is way out in front. He's just making the turn from Route 7 onto the bridge. Second place belongs to number 5. Let's see . . . that would be high-school senior Allen Barnes.

"Right behind him is a bunch of about ten racers. It looks like the first racers will be crossing the finish line in fifteen or twenty minutes. Number 18, Paul Kenyon, is still in first place. He's riding one of the fastest races of his career."

As Paul turned onto the bridge, he

glanced ahead. He saw the long up-grade into town. A look behind told him he had built up an easy lead. He could see the bikers beginning to come around the curve. They were far behind him. He smiled. He knew he was making good time.

And then, *"hiss-s-s-ss."* Paul heard the air escape from his tire. He felt the wobble in his front wheel. He dismounted instantly.

"Broken glass! Why do people use highways as garbage cans?" he grumbled angrily. At the same time, he blamed himself. That quick backward glance to admire his lead may have cost him the race. He should have been watching for glass instead.

"Now the *real* race starts," Paul muttered. And he began to change the tire. Suddenly, all those Saturdays at the Bicycle Barn paid off. Paul had the old tire off and the new one out from under the bike seat before the nearest racer caught up with him. He concentrated on what he was doing.

"Watch the glass!" he shouted, as Allen neared him.

"Thanks. Gee, I'm sorry, Paul!" panted Allen as he shifted gears.

"Don't feel sorry for me until you cross the finish line!" Paul fitted the tire around the rim and began pumping. The line of racers began to pass him.

The helicopter hovered overhead. The sports announcer continued his report. "This is Arnie McKnight bringing you the final minutes of the

The helicopter hovered overhead.

bicycle race. Well, sports fans, it's a brand-new race. Paul Kenyon appears to be out of the race. He's below me now, at the foot of the Route 10 hill. He seems to be fixing a flat tire. Tough luck, Paul. Let's look now at the new first-place racer, Allen Barnes..."

At the finish line, Alice Kenyon sighed. She turned off Arnie's broadcast. She wondered when Paul would enter his next race.

Paul finished changing the tire. He jumped back on his bike, and started pedaling. It was hard to start an uphill climb with no momentum. It was hard to pass seven or eight racers. But it was even harder to imagine losing this race.

Paul flattened himself over his bike

and pedaled. Slowly, he passed one bike after another. Just as he reached the top of the hill, he shot past Allen Barnes. This time, he did not stop to admire his lead. He raced for the finish line two blocks ahead.

"This is Arnie McKnight, coming to you live from the finish line. Here comes the first biker now. Sports fans, you're not going to believe this. It's number 18, Paul Kenyon! Let's see if we can get a few words with him. Paul? Paul, I'm amazed! I was sure you were out of the race. Fifteen minutes ago, you were changing a tire! Could you say a few words to our radio audience?"

"Well, Arnie, I just won *two* important races. I won my last bike race and my first repair race. I'll be retiring from bike racing now and opening my own repair shop. I'm sure I can't be beat for speedy repairs! And I think my wife Alice will be glad to have all the bikes out of our dining room."

Behind him, Allen Barnes grinned. Second-place money wasn't so bad, after all. It wouldn't put him through college. But it would buy a couple of textbooks.

Out on Route 86, Jim and Mike sighed. Oh, well—there was always next year.

59

Terror on the Ice

Ed fumbled with the laces on his new skates. His fingers were cold and stiff. The wind blew the dusting of snow off the pond and into his face.

"Come on, Ed. Let's warm up! I'll race you around the pond." Brian grabbed Ed's hat and stuffed it into his back pocket. Ed zoomed after him.

It felt good to be back on skates after the long summer. He stretched, trying to snatch his hat out of Brian's pocket. His fingers brushed the red pompom, but Brian sped forward, just out of reach.

Halfway around the pond, a whistle interrupted the chase. Brian skated off to the goalie cage waving Ed's hat.

"Thanks, Ed. Now I'm all warmed up!" yelled Brian, pulling the hat down over his ears.

"How can a goalie skate so fast?" wondered Ed. He coasted with his mittens over his ears. The season was just starting, and Ed could tell that he was out of condition. *It's a good thing I decided to put in some extra practice time out here at the pond,* he thought to himself. The tryouts for the team were next week at the town rink. Ed needed to get into shape before then.

"Lose your hat?" hooted Jake. Jake played center.

"No, I'm just a nice guy. Goalies with warm ears make more saves."

"Maybe so, Ed. But let's see if wings with *cold* ears score more hat tricks!" laughed Jake. He skated past Ed into position. Jake blew his whistle again to get the game going.

"On your left! On your left!" someone screamed as the action started.

Ed couldn't spot the puck, but his skates were already taking him to the left. The afternoon shadows made it hard to see anything on the ice. He leaned to stop the puck before it went

He leaned to stop the puck.

out of bounds. The edge of his skate caught on a bubble in the ice. He fell forward.

With horror, Ed felt icy pond water instead of solid ice as his shoulder hit the surface. He gasped. His mouth was full of water. The early winter ice cracked and gave way at the force of his fall. He tried to yell, but the water in his mouth and nose made yelling impossible.

Everyone was talking and yelling at once. Ed could see his friends skating toward him, shouting to each other, pointing their sticks. He wondered how long he had been in the water. Ten seconds? The edge of the ice was crumbling in his hands. He kicked his legs, trying to tread water. But it was no use. His skates were dragging him down. The ice kept breaking off in his hands.

The sudden blast of Jake's whistle stopped everything for an instant.

"Stop skating. Stop right where you are. If you skate any closer, you'll all fall in!" Jake's voice snapped through the cold air.

"But we can't let him drown!" someone cried.

"Of course we can't," hollered Brian. "But Jake is right. We won't save him if we fall in too."

Ed began to panic. How long had he been in the freezing water now? How long could he last?

"Line up," ordered Brian. "Lie down. Grab the ankles of the guy in front. Hang on, Ed! We're coming. Try to float, Ed. Keep your eyes on us.

Don't give up!"

Brian kept talking to Ed as the team followed his orders. A long chain of skaters inched toward Ed on their bellies. The ice rumbled and shifted. But it didn't break.

Brian's voice sounded far away to Ed. He had to force his eyes to stay open. *Keep looking. Keep kicking. Keep trying to stay afloat,* he told himself. It was getting harder and harder to think. The edge of the ice broke off again in his hands. Ed's fingers were freezing, but he grabbed the ice again. The skaters crawled closer. Could he hold on? His eyes focused on something red.

"Hey, Ed! Don't you want your hat back?" Brian's voice sounded suddenly closer. Brian waved the hat in one hand and pushed his hockey stick

Brian pushed his hockey stick toward Ed.

toward Ed with his other hand. Brian's voice and the waving red hat kept Ed's eyes open a few more seconds. Finally, the hockey stick reached Ed's fingers.

"OK, now, Ed. Listen carefully." Brian's voice filled the air. "Grab that stick. Try to hook your elbow around it. Right. Good man! Now team! Hang on! Guys at the end, pull the chain back!"

Ed felt the hockey stick pull him forward, but the ice cracked under him. Ed's hands slipped.

"Kick, Ed!" shouted Brian. "Get those skates up! Hang on!"

Ed tightened his grip and tried to kick his legs up to the surface. At last, he felt solid ice sliding under his chest. He kicked harder. He heard shouts and cheers. Brian's hands locked around his wrists so he didn't have to hang on anymore. He felt himself sliding over the ice to safety. He closed his eyes.

His friends' voices faded out as Ed gave in to an overpowering need for sleep.

"Quick! He's going into shock," shouted Jake.

"I'll go for help!" offered Brian.

"We have to try to warm him up," Jake said.

Hours later, Ed opened his eyes again. He heard Jake and Brian talking. But the white world of ice and snow had become the white of a warm hospital room.

"Hi, guys," said Ed. "Sorry to interrupt practice like that."

*"I'll do almost anything for a nice hat
like this."*

"Don't mention it," grinned Brian with relief. "But next time, don't throw yourself into the game quite so hard, OK?"

Ed noticed his red hat pulled down over Brian's ears.

"Well," said Ed gratefully. "I guess we found out that goalies with warm ears *do* make more saves. Thanks, Brian."

"Any time!" smiled Brian. "I'll do almost anything for a nice hat like this."

Bear Mountain Mystery

Janet caught up with Heidi on the trail.

"Whew!" She kicked off her skis and dropped down on the snow. "Doesn't this hill go anyplace but up?" she asked.

Heidi was standing over her. She laughed. "You're doing two things wrong," she said. "Your parka is too heavy for cross-country skiing. And you need to use a softer wax to keep from slipping."

Janet dug into her pocket for her wax. The newspaper clipping they had brought with them fell out with the wax. She reread it for the tenth time:

"Pearson, Vermont. Many town residents have been complaining about low-flying aircraft. The mysterious craft sounds like a helicopter and flies late at night. It passes over the town and heads out over Bear Mountain. Nearby airfields deny having flights at night. Because the craft flies without lights, state police are investigating."

The race lasted about a quarter of a mile.

Nothing ever happened in Pearson, Vermont. So, having a mysterious object flying around was a real challenge. And that's what Janet and Heidi were doing on Bear Mountain. They had planned to go cross-country skiing anyway. Why not ski up the trail on Bear Mountain and look around?

When Janet had rested, they set out again. "There's an old hunting cabin near the top of the mountain," Heidi said. "I'll race you to it."

The race lasted about a quarter of a mile. Then they both collapsed, gasping for breath. They were on the edge of a clearing.

"I'm hungry," Janet said at last.

"Me too," Heidi agreed. "Let's find a sunny spot and have lunch." They began to circle the big field in front of them.

"Look at the funny snowdrifts," Janet said. "The snow is almost gone in the middle of the field. But it's real deep out here. It looks kind of like craters on the moon."

"Or like whirlpools," suggested Heidi.

"*Or drifts caused by helicopters landing!*" Janet shouted. "The helicopter is landing here!"

"You know, Janet," Heidi said slowly, "you may be right. But stop shouting. There may be something fishy going on here. Let's see if we can find out what."

They circled the field once more on their skis. Suddenly, both girls spotted a snowmobile trail. They hadn't noticed it before. It led from the "crater" to the edge of the field. Then it disappeared into the woods. The girls decided to follow it.

Within fifty yards, they came to the old hunting cabin. The shades on the window were drawn. The doors were locked. There was nothing unusual about that. But the snowmobile tracks ended here, and they didn't go any-place else.

"Snowmobiles in a cabin?" Janet asked.

"Possible, but unusual," Heidi said. "Let's try to see inside."

"We can't," said Janet. "The shades are down." They walked around the cabin. Then Janet noticed a gleam of light coming from inside. The girls stopped and took a closer look.

Heidi found a crack and put her eye to it.

There were cracks in the cabin wall. They were small cracks, but were just wide enough so that light from the sun could shine through. The light was shining on something inside the cabin.

Heidi found a crack and put her eye to it. "Come here, Janet," she called. "This whole setup is starting to make sense now."

Janet looked through the crack. "The place is full of snowmobiles!" she said. "They must be stealing them, and then bringing them here to repaint them. Look at the cans of spray paint in the corner."

"Exactly!" Heidi said. "So now we know what the helicopter folks are doing!"

"The next stop is the state-police

barracks," Janet said.

"Next stop is nowhere," a voice said behind them. Another skier had come up quietly behind them. Unfortunately, this skier wasn't out for a day of fun. He looked mean. And he had a shotgun cradled in his arms.

"Kick the skis off," he ordered. "We're going inside the cabin. Tonight, we'll go for a little helicopter ride."

The girls were terrified. But they decided they weren't going into the cabin. They both got the same idea at the same time. They pretended to poke at the toe-latches on their skis with their ski poles. Then, without warning, they lifted their poles like spears. They lunged at the man. The sharp points found their mark. The man fell backward, and the gun exploded. Before he could recover, Janet and Heidi were into the woods and skiing down the mountain.

They had a good head start. But they weren't good enough skiers to stay ahead. The man had gotten up, reloaded his gun, and was after them. It was like a dream. There wasn't a sound except the swish of skis on snow. The deadly game was being played out in silence.

Then there was a sharp turn in the trail. Janet couldn't make it. She screamed as her skis went out from under her. Heidi was right behind and tumbled on top of her.

The man skidded to a stop and slung the shotgun off his shoulder. "I've had it with you kids," he shouted at them. He leveled the gun. His finger was on the trigger.

*Suddenly, a snowmobile seemed to appear
out of nowhere.*

Suddenly, a snowmobile seemed to appear out of nowhere. It was racing down the trail without making a sound. When it hit the man, he was thrown off the trail and into a snowbank. This time, when the gun exploded, the girls thought they were dead for sure.

But they weren't. When they were able to open their eyes, they looked into the face of a man with a blond mustache. "Are you kids okay?" he asked. They felt themselves and shook their heads "yes"—no broken bones, no bullet holes.

"State police," he said. "Corporal Baines. I was on my way up the other side of the mountain. We've been watching that hunting cabin, too. It's the only place we could figure a helicopter might land. Then I heard the shotgun blast. When I got to the clearing, I had a glimpse of what was going on. So I turned my engine off and slid downhill after you."

"What about the helicopter?" Heidi asked.

"We'll stake out the cabin," Corporal Baines said. "With luck, we'll get them tonight."

Janet sighed. "Can we go back to Pearson now?" she asked.

"You bet," Heidi said. "Good old Pearson, where nothing ever happens!"

Broken Promises

Terry braked his motorcycle. He skidded to a stop at the top of the hill. *This can't be right,* he said to himself. He took off his helmet and looked down into the valley. There was no road in sight. He pulled a map out of his pocket. The map showed a county road, Route 63. The road ran down the center of the valley.

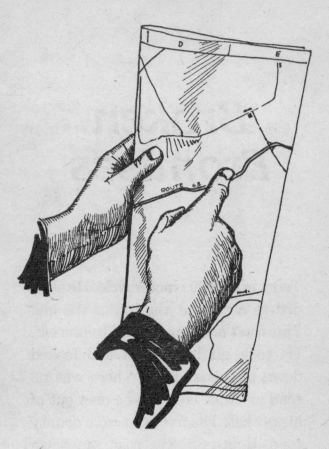

The map showed a county road, Route 63.

It must be hidden by trees, he told himself. He put his helmet on and looked back. His friends had spotted him. He waited for them, stuffing the map back in his pocket. It was a beautiful day for a trail ride. The spring sun had melted the snow and dried the mud.

As the other two motorcycles reached him, Terry gunned his engine. He made a wide sliding turn and took off down the logging road. Bob roared by, weaving back and forth. Marty crowded past on the other side. His red jacket flashed out of sight.

Marty had a faster machine. But Bob was a better rider. Marty was always fooling around. He was Mr. Stunt Man. Bob didn't go in for that kind of thing. He just rode fast. He

He made a sliding turn.

never seemed to lose control.

The trail turned to loose rocks and dropped steeply. Terry shifted down. His bike rattled over the bumpy surface. Terry fought to keep control of his machine. Then he saw Marty's bike. It was lying on its side. Where was Marty?

Terry skidded to a stop. Something red caught his eye. It was Marty. He lay in a heap, about fifty feet down. He must have been thrown from the bike. His body looked crumpled, and he wasn't moving.

Terry scrambled down the slope. "Marty!" he shouted. "Are you all right?" No answer. He could hear the whine of Bob's engine climbing back up the trail.

Terry knelt beside his friend. Marty was still breathing. There wasn't much blood, but one arm was bent where it shouldn't be.

Bob scrambled down the hill beside him. "Look at that arm," he said, giving a low whistle. "It looks like he has an extra elbow."

"We have to get him out of here," said Terry.

Marty groaned. His eyelids fluttered. He tried to move, but passed out again.

"That arm must really hurt," said Bob. "Are you sure we should move him?"

"Unless there's something wrong with his back, we have to. No ambulance is going to make it up here. It's up to us to get him out."

Marty woke up again. "Is my machine all right?" he asked.

"Your machine?" exploded Bob. "We're more worried about your body right now!"

"How about wiggling your toes for us?" said Terry.

Marty wiggled. His legs and left arm seemed fine. It was just his right arm they had to worry about. Terry didn't even like looking at it. Then he noticed something else wiggling— Marty's ears!

"Hey, Marty! You must be in worse shape than I thought. We said wiggle your toes, not your ears!"

Marty managed a smile.

Terry took off his T-shirt. He ripped it into strips. Bob knotted the strips together, and made a sling for Marty's arm.

"OK, buddy," said Terry. "Up-sy

91

daisy." He half-lifted Marty to his feet. "One foot in front of the other now." Terry kept talking. "Give me some help." He was afraid Marty would pass out again.

Up on top, Bob was ready and waiting. He had mounted his bike and started the engine. Terry helped Marty get onto the back, behind Bob. He buckled Marty's belt through Bob's belt loops. The belt would help keep him on. Then Terry started his own machine. He rode behind, to keep an eye on Marty.

Bob rode very slowly. He tried to miss the bumps. But this road was nothing but bumps. Marty was hanging on to Bob with his left arm. Bob could hear him groan with pain.

Finally, the road widened and

leveled out. Terry spotted an old house. The yard was overgrown, and the porch needed paint. But there might be a telephone. He ran to the door. An old woman opened it. Bob saw her nod as Terry talked. A moment later, he was back, unbuckling Marty and Bob.

Marty's face was grayish white. He slumped down. Bob and Terry half-carried him inside. While Bob called for help, Terry led Marty to a couch. The woman wrapped Marty in a quilt.

"How did you boys get way out here?" she asked.

"We've been trail riding, Mrs. Forbes," explained Terry. "We were coming down the logging road there, looking for Route 63." He pulled out his map and pointed to a red line.

"Were you now?" said Mrs. Forbes with a chuckle. "Well, then, it's no wonder you got in some trouble. You must have an old map. Route 63 doesn't exist. It never has, except on paper. A couple of years ago, some big shot wanted to get elected governor. He promised us that road. He made it seem so real that the state even put it on the map. A couple of bulldozers pushed dirt around for a few days. The man got elected. The map got printed. But Route 63 never got built.

"To tell the truth," she went on, "I'm glad it didn't. I hate traffic. And it would have spoiled the trail riding," she said, with a twinkle in her eye.

The wail of a siren split the air. "There's the police," said Mrs. Forbes. "They'll get Marty to a hospital." She turned to Marty. "Take care of that arm now, you hear?"

"I will, Mrs. Forbes," said Marty.

"And thanks," added Terry. "We'll all come back to visit. And that's a real promise—not just one on paper!"